Symphony no. 8 in B-minor

To the memory of
Charles M. Schulz,
my BECAUSE
—M.W.

For my Mama, Baba,
and Laolao, BECAUSE
they believed in me
—A.R.

First Edition, March 2019
10 9 8 7 6 5 4 3 2 1
FAC-029191-18341
Printed in Malaysia

This book is set in Harmonia Sans Pro/Monotype
Designed by Tyler Nevins
Title lettering by Molly Jacques
Special thanks to music consultant Peter Rofé, Los Angeles Philharmonic

Library of Congress Cataloging-in-Publication Data

Names: Willems, Mo, author. | Ren, Amber, illustrator.
Title: Because / words by Mo Willems ; pictures by Amber Ren.
Description: First edition. | New York : Hyperion Books For Children, 2019. |
Summary: A series of events, some seemingly very insignificant, lead to a
young girl attending a life-changing concert.
Identifiers: LCCN 2017046403 | ISBN 9781368019019 (hardcover)
Subjects: | CYAC: Musicians—Fiction. | Concerts—Fiction. |
Serendipity—Fiction.
Classification: LCC PZ7.W65535 Bec 2019 | DDC [E]—dc23
LC record available at https://lccn.loc.gov/2017046403

Reinforced binding

Visit hyperionbooksforchildren.com and pigeonpresents.com

BECAUSE

Score by **Mo Willems**
Performance by **Amber Ren**

HYPERION BOOKS FOR CHILDREN / New York

This is how it happened:

Because a man named Ludwig wrote
beautiful music—

a man named Franz was inspired
to create his own.

Because many years later, people wanted to hear
Franz's beautiful music—

they formed an orchestra.

Because a man had practiced
since he was a kid—

he was asked to join.

Because a woman studied night and day—
she, too, was asked to play.

Because many others loved and practiced their instruments—

there were enough musicians.

Because someone created a poster about Franz's music—

tickets were sold.

Because the train conductor stopped
the train at the grand concert hall—
the orchestra conductor arrived.

Because the orchestra librarian
had copies of the score—

the orchestra rehearsed.

Because workers checked the lights and the seats and swept the floors— the grand hall was ready.

Because the time
had come—

the ushers opened the doors.

Because someone's uncle
caught a cold—

someone's aunt had an extra ticket
for someone special.

Because the usher helped the aunt
and her special guest—

they found their seats.

Because everyone was there to hear beautiful music—
it was quiet.

In row C, seat 14—

sat the girl with
the uncle's ticket.

She heard the beautiful music written by the man named Franz—

and it changed her.

The girl was changed.

From that moment on, the girl learned everything
she could about music—

because it fed her.

Soon, she started to write music, too—

because, like Franz, the young woman had something to share.

Over time, the woman became very good—
because she worked very hard.

One night, her music was discovered—
because she was also very lucky.

Then she was invited to perform her music
at the grand concert hall—

because so many people wanted to hear it.

Her composition was
dedicated to the uncle in
row C, seat 14—

because it was his ticket that brought her here.

And that night, someone else was changed.

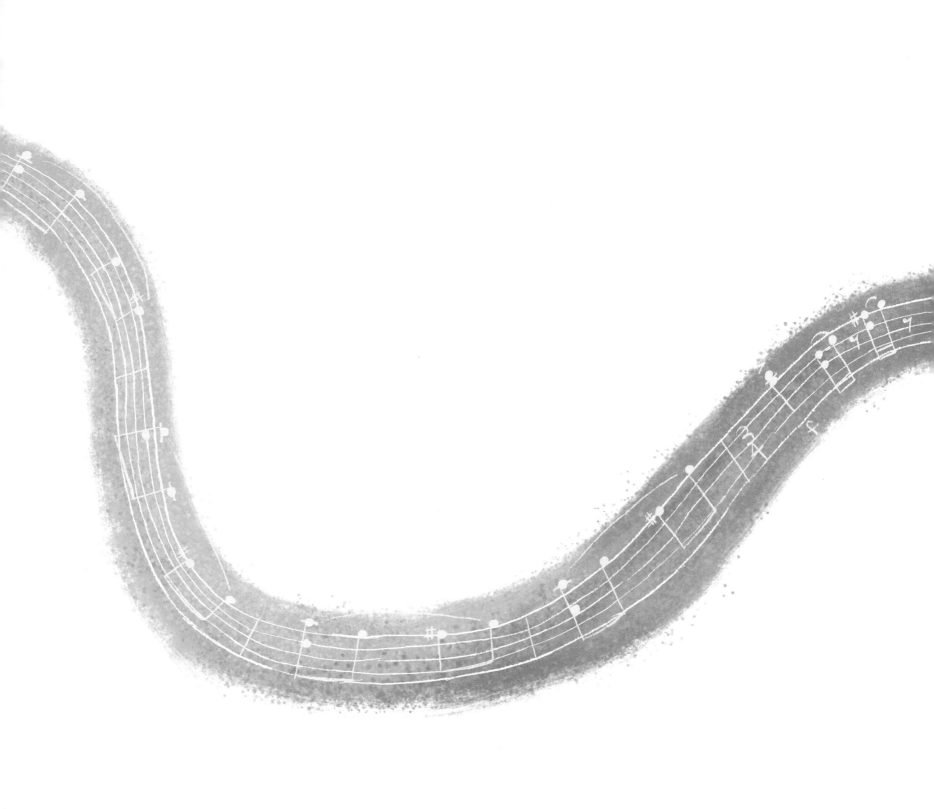

That is how it happens.

The Cold

Hilary Purrington